The Club

Brian Leon Lee

ISBN: 9781521243879

The Author

The author was born in Manchester. On leaving school, a period in accountancy was followed by a teaching career in Primary Education.

He has published, as Brian Leo Lee, several children's short stories including the popular Bouncey the Elf and Mr Tripsy.

Trimefirst, a science fiction novella, was published under the name of Brian Leon Lee in 2012, followed by the fantasy novel, Domain of the Netherworld, in 2013.

Now retired and living in South Yorkshire.

By Brian Leo Lee
(Children's stories)
Bouncey the Elf and Friends Bedtime Stories
Just Bouncey
Bouncey the Elf and Friends Meet Again
Bouncey the Elf and Friends (Box Set)

Four Tales from Sty-Pen

Mr Tripsy's Trip
Mr Tripsy's Boat Trip

By Brian Leon Lee
Trimefirst
Domain of the Netherworld

All available as eBooks and Paperbacks

http://www.bounceytheelf.co.uk

Check for Free selected
eBooks
Brian Leo / Leon Lee
@ smashwords.com

For Rita

1

'Can we come to order. I say, can we make a start. We're fifteen minutes late as it is.'

The Chair of Harlston WMC, Yorkshire, Dave Carpenter (ex overman at the Harlston pit) banged his pewter pint tankard on the table-top, forgetting that he had just had a refill, and spilt a good mouthful onto his notes.

'Shit, look what you've made me do.'

Loud guffaws echoed in the big concert room.

'Tonight's emergency meeting called by the club committee has a quorum, so we are legit,' he said as he looked at the tables set out in front of him and his officers for the meeting, most of which were empty.

'Steady, Dave,' called out Budd Rackette, a retired miner. His hearing had declined years ago and he spoke without realizing that he usually deafened those sat near him.

'Tha' knows that you haven't paid for that, so there's no need to wash table top with some of it.'

More guffaws from the floor.

Dave grinned and dabbed at the spilt beer with a tissue, before taking a gulp of his drink.

'Okay; now I have your attention I want to say that this is not a happy situation for our club. In fact, to coin a phrase, we're up to our necks in it.'

The members suddenly went quiet.

There had been rumours. There are always rumours in villages but the tone of the chairman went home.

Hands reached for drinks. One or two chairs scraped the floor as their occupants shuffled in anticipation of bad news.

The Chairman looked to one side and pointed to the club treasurer, Fred Notte, (Ex Pit manager's assistant).

'You will remember or at least most of you will, that last year Fred loaned the club six thousand pounds of his own money to pay for the repair and refurbishing of our snooker table and lighting, damaged by a visiting team of so called lady snooker players.'

'Yesh, I certainly do,' mumbled Wilf Caul (ex lamp-man at the pit), from the far side of the table, where other committee members sat. He had, as usual, forgotten to put his top set of teeth in for the meeting.

He took off his pebble like glasses and waved them in the air, his heavy jowls wobbling in sympathy.

'It was a dishgraceful exhibition. I mean it's not as though they were young ladiesh either. When they beat our men'sh team, four to one and started to dance about shouting, *don't you know how to use your cue ladsh,* all hell broke loosh.'

'Yeah,' Budd called out. 'But who was tha' idiot that put on that strip music?'

'Does it matter now,' said Zoe Chatts. 'Four *ladies* in high heels doing a strip dance on the snooker table before anyone knew what was going on.'

'Or off,' sniggered Budd.

'Mister Chairman,' Wes Booke, a local Teacher's union official interrupted, 'Can we please get back to the matter at hand.'

'Hear, hear,' said Maggie Stepp. 'I want to know if this club is going to close or not.'

A loud clatter of coins dropping into the bandit pay-out tray made everyone turn to look at the machine by the door.

Steve Woolfe was hunched over it. Still broad in the shoulder after twenty years of shoveling coal onto a conveyer belt, he looked over at them with a cheeky grin and waved.

'The drinks will be on me,' he called. 'That's if I don't put it all back.'

'For God's sake, give it a rest Steve and come over here.'

The Chairman wasn't amused by the way things where going.

He waited patiently well as long as it took him to drink three-quarters of a pint and for Steve to limp over to a nearby table (a coal rail tub had run over his foot years earlier) and called to the club steward, Barney Drinkwater to bring him a pint.

'As I was saying, and thank you Wes for bringing us back to the agenda.'

Wes sat up at the mention of his name. He liked nothing more than being involved in a meeting. He turned to his neighbour, Len Glazer and smirked at him.

'I'm going to let our secretary, Walt Penn (ex pit time-keeper), explain the current situation, said the Chairman.

'Okay Walt, it's all yours.'

Walt started to push his chair back in order to stand up, when Eric Elver, still in his Rail uniform called out.

'Sit thee down Walt. We can all see you from here.'

Eric nodded to his four mates sitting at his table, all drivers like him and making up for lost time. The table was covered with empty pint glasses. Unfortunately, for Eric, as he nodded, his smart looking blonde hairstyle suddenly slipped over his forehead. (It was a wig).

His mates erupted with laughter. 'Ey up,' one cried out. 'Eric's cat's woke up.'

Budd Rackette leaned over and whispered to Zoe's husband, Don, (ex pit electrician), sitting next to him. 'I didn't know that Eric had a cat and what the 'ell is it doin' on his eead?'

Of course everyone heard Budd and either laughed out loud or stifled a snigger as best they could.

The Chairman groaned out loud. 'Jeez, for God's sake can we get a move on. We'll be here all night at this rate.'

After a few coughs and the wiping of an eye or two, things calmed down enough for the Secretary to read from his notes.

'The problem is that we're more or less broke,' he began. 'The club can't at the moment pay back the loan owing to Fred, our treasurer. He has very kindly said he will give us more time to see if we can come up with a way to find the money due to him.'

'Good on you,' Fred,' called Maggie looking over at him and giving him a big smile.

The Treasurer looked down sheepishly and then nodded a silent thank you to her. He would make sure that she would be pleased with what he would give her later on that night in his car before she went home.

Unfortunately, the Secretary's voice lacked that certain something that would hold a meeting's attention. He droned on about the lack of turnover in the bar caused largely, he said, by the effects of the eighty-four strike and the subsequent pit closures in the area with the inevitable loss of jobs.

'This,' he added, 'Has been made worse by the supermarkets discounting alcohol by so much that it undercuts pub and club prices and though we try to be competitive, people are not coming out as they once did. Playback TV hasn't helped either. The Railway Tavern

---

10

and the Bulls Head on the other side of the village have both closed recently as you all well know.'

Walt paused and looked at the meeting, which had become much more attentive. Having suddenly realized that things were really more serious then they had thought.

'Drop the price of beer then,' shouted Budd, to much applause from his mates.

Walt peered at Budd over his glasses.

'Our bar prices are the best in the village, fifty pence a pint better than the Harlston Arms but it still isn't enough.....'

'Bloody hell,' interrupted Ged 'Lofty' Carr the village taxi driver, as he stood up. (All five foot of him).

'We're going to close aren't we Dave? Admit it Dave. Admit it. Go on tell us. Thirty years I've been a member here. Christ, what will I do. The missus will kick me out if I stay in more than Tuesday night.'

Len Glazer laughed out loud. 'Never mind Lofty, you can always go to the Harlston Arms. That is if you have a suit. You know how 'stuck up' that lot are.'

The Harlston Arms was the haunt of the local Rotary Business and Commerce Club.

Lofty, in his tracksuit and baseball cap, lifted two fingers at Len, to jeers from Eric's table.

'Well then, Dave what is it,' he said. 'Are we done as a club or not?'

'Yeah,' cried Maggie Stepp, 'We all want to know too.'

Chairman Dave Carpenter raised a hand and got to his feet.

'Calm down Lofty. Calm down,' he said quietly.

'Walt was just about to tell all of you.' Dave turned and gave Walt a long glaring look and sat down.

Getting the message, Walt pulled at his tie knot. It suddenly felt very tight. He daren't loosen it and so he coughed and took a sip of his shandy, wishing it was something stronger.

'Well. Yes, yes that's right Mr Chairman. I was just about to get to the real point of this emergency meeting,' Walt muttered.

'Go on then, what is it,' called out Budd loud enough for anyone earwigging in the taproom.

'And speak up, I'm.....'

'As deaf as a bloomin doorpost,' shouted Len, to more jeers from Eric and his mates.

'Well, I... I have some good news and some bad news,' announced the club secretary.

'He's going to get a round in,' shouted Eric Elver.

'More like it's for a pint and a box of straws,' Len Glazer said, winking at Wes, who looked away pretending he hadn't heard him.

'Lads, lads. Give the Secretary a bit of slack. Okay.'

The Chairman nodded to Walt who took a quick sip of his shandy and went on.

'The good news is that the Club has been made an offer. Chaz Bolton, you know, who has interests in the local rugby club as well as the sports and social club outside Castleford, feels that he could develop our club site.'

'What! Knock down our club! No way. No way!' cried Budd Rackette, his voice echoing round the concert room.

Questions were shouted to the Secretary but Wes Booke surprised them getting in first.

'That's the good news, is it?' Wes stood up, he felt this was his moment.

Mr Tripsy's Trip
Brian Leo Lee

eBook
Paperback
smashwords.com
www.amazon.co.uk
Apple Books

'How the hell is knocking down our club good news.'

The Chairman banged his empty pewter hard on the table. 'Quiet please. One at a time, let Walt answer Wes's question.'

Walt felt sweat forming on his forehead and dabbed at it with his handkerchief.

'Listen, it's not what you think.'

'Oh yeah, what is then,' called Maggie Stepp.

Taking a deep breath, Walt tried again.

'Mr Bolton has offered to pay all outstanding debts, which will include of course the amount we owe Fred and the substantial amount we owe the Brewery. He doesn't want to knock it down.'

'What then?' asked Zoe Chatts who had been listening patiently, 'What happens to the Club? You know, who will run it if we don't?'

'May I Mr Chairman,' Fred Notte looked at Dave Carpenter, who nodded.

Fred stood up and waved his hands for quiet.

'As Treasurer I've been worried sick for months about the finances of our club. You want the honest truth.'

He paused and looked at everyone in the eye. He knew everyone. Been to school with most of them as well.

'If we don't find a buyer inside of the next few weeks, this club goes to the wall.'

Silence greeted his words, and then Wes Booke spoke up. 'So what are the terms of this so-called sale?'

'Quite simple really,' replied the Treasurer. 'We will be guaranteed a seven-year lease to run the club as before but we will not own anything because we will have to sign over the deeds of the club.'

'What then?' asked Wes quietly.

'The club closes,' said the Treasurer.

'My God, what a choice,' cried Lofty, speaking for everyone.

'So, the good news is we have seven more years,' said Wes Booke. 'And the bad....'

'We shut in two weeks,' said Walt, his voice breaking with emotion.

'Mr Chairman.' Paul Flite (ex shot-firer at the pit) and Vice-Chairman had been busy for the past half hour, rolling a stash of thin cigarettes, whilst listening to the goings on.

'I move that the question be put to the members now. Whether we like it or not, we have to decide tonight.'

'What do you mean?' asked Maggie Stepp. 'It has to be done tonight.'

The Chairman raised a hand. 'It's like this. You, the members of the club actually own it. This quorum has the right to vote on the sale or transfer of the ownership of this club and you need to do it tonight, otherwise Mr Bolton will call the deal off and we will close in two weeks. I'm sorry but the Committee has to recommend that we accept the terms of the offer.'

The hall was silent, people looked at each other then looked away.

Walt Penn the club secretary stood up and said in a quiet voice, 'Would those in favour of the motion please raise a hand.'

All the committee members raised a hand and then, slowly one after the other, the members present raised a hand. It was unanimous.

The spell broke and the various people on different tables got to their feet and began to mingle. A hubbub of conversations echoed round the concert room. Shock and disbelief etched most faces. There was a rush to the bar led by the railway driver, Eric Elver.

The bar steward, Barney Drinkwater, smartly turned out as usual, his thinning hair slicked back, bow-tie, white shirt and paisley patterned waist-coat giving him an air of sophistication not often found in a WMC, walked into the Concert Room bar from the taproom along the connecting passage when he heard the commotion of the meeting breaking up.

Already forewarned about the possibilities of the club's future, he had previously pulled half a dozen pints in anticipation of the rush.

Eric appreciated the gesture by nearly drinking his first pint by the time Budd, Lofty and Steve arrived at the bar followed by a group arguing that maybe they had been too hasty.

Bit late now, Wes Booke was heard to be saying.

Zoe and Maggie sat together waiting for the others to be served.

The committee stayed where they were, huddled round their table when Wilf Caul stood on a chair and shouted as loud as he could.

'Don't forget the Bingo startsh in fifteen minutesh. Will some of you give a hand in moving these tablesh back pleash.'

'Oh come on Zoe.' said Maggie, 'Let's give the poor sod a hand with the tables, otherwise we'll never get the Bingo started on time.'

2

Paul Flite, stood pint in hand and one elbow on the concert room bar already feeling much better.

A quick fag on the club doorstep. My God was he gasping for one. The bloody meeting seemed to last for ever. He'd actually run out of baccy. He had rolled so many whilst listening to the death sentence of his club. *Well*, he thought, *more of a delayed execution really*.

Then his mate Larry Wallerton had come from the taproom and cadged a cig from him.

'You know what,' Larry had said, 'Old Bill Harpson's cat nearly got into my loft last night.'

Larry was a pigeon fancier too and kept his pigeons in a shed known locally as a loft.

'Luckily,' he went on, 'I saw the little bastard and winged it with me catapult. It were only a bit of muck but you should have seen the bugger jump. I don't think it will be back in a hurry.'

'Dam nuisance cats,' Paul replied. 'Cost me a fortune in chicken wire to keep them out of my loft. Worth it though.'

Larry nodded in agreement and said, 'I don't know what I'd do without me birds.'

They both took a drag on their ciggies, minds miles away thinking about winning the next pigeon race.

'Anyway,' Paul stopped daydreaming and took a sup of his pint as he looked at Eric Elvin, perched precariously on a bar stool next to him.

Eric by now was rocking a bit on his seat. *Must ease off a bit*, he thought to himself as he tried to concentrate on what Paul was saying.

'It must have been a Whit Bank Holiday weekend,' continued Paul, 'It was quite warm.'

'We were walking home from the nightclub; Tha knows the one in Crosspark. Me and Shay Kelly. It must have been well after one in the morning. A right belly-full we'd had. I can tell you.'

Paul had another drink and went on.

'We had just reached the roundabout near the canal. Tha knows the one.'

Eric nodded gently and gripped the bar tightly.

'Well, would you bloody believe it. Just then a soddin' lorry came chugging round it, right slow like. It was a clapped out flat-bed.

As we shifted out of the way, Shay shouted, 'Quick jump on. It's going our way.'

Like a frigging idiot I did. We landed on scraps of old canvas so we snuck under them hoping the driver wouldn't see us. Then, what with the beer and the rocking of the lorry we fell asleep.'

Paul paused to drain his glass and asked Barney for a refill.

Eric shook his head indicating that he was okay at the moment. Actually he daren't let go of the bar it was swaying so much.

'You know what Eric?' asked Paul.

Eric shook his head and wished he hadn't.

'We ended up in chuffin Newcastle. Newcastle I ask you. It took us another eight hours to hitch home. I lost a shift because of that pillock. Well I couldn't really blame him could I. I was as pissed as he was. Mind you I don't go drinking with him anymore.'

'Very wise,' said Eric, suddenly realizing that he needed the gents too.

Then Paul saw Wilf Caul waving madly to him.

'God,' he groaned, 'Is it Bingo time all ready. Okay, okay Wilf, I'm coming.'

3

At the far end of the concert room by the stage, was a small booth. All lighting and the sound system could be controlled from it. There was also room for a Bingo cage, which was full of the numbered coloured balls - ninety and the number check-tray.

Thanks to the efforts of Zoe and Maggie plus four early Bingo players, the tables were made ready for what many had thought might be the last Bingo the club would hold.

So instead of the regular dozen or so players, an extra twenty or so people had turned up, mostly as usual, of the senior citizen age group.

Wilf was over the moon. 'Thish is the besht turnout since New Yearsh Eve,' he said to Paul, rubbing his hands.

'I had to ashk Barney for some more prizesh, jush in cashhe we ran thort.'

Paul nodded. He was as surprised as Wilf at the extra numbers. He looked round as the tables filled up, waving to the nearest ones he knew, as the chatter and bustle became louder.

The regulars had great fat bingo markers of different colours. They usually bought two or three bingo cards and used a different colour for each card.

Not too far from the booth Paul saw Steve Woolfe with his usual four cards. He rarely went home without a prize. Sitting next to Steve were the four rail drivers and Eric Elver. Eric was holding his head in his hands. *He looks rough,* thought Paul.

'Come on,' he told himself. 'Get on with it.'

So he sat down next to Wilf, who by now had sorted the Bingo cage and check-tray to his satisfaction and pressed a button to switch on the microphone and sound system.

'Let's give them a bit of music while they get settled,' he said to Wilf.

Wilf nodded and gave the Bingo cage a few turns by rotating the handle. The balls rattled around nicely.

Paul hit the play button of the CD player, which was linked to the concert room speakers and the lively sound of 'Peggy Sue' pulsed out of the speakers.

The effect was electric. Within moments couples led by Maggie and Zoe were dancing between the tables. Many more joined in the song. The concert hall was alive with movement and faces all around the hall were smiling and laughing.

Paul joined in by making hand jive gestures, his head bobbing in time to the rhythm.

Even Wilf couldn't stop himself from tapping his feet. Then he whispered to Paul, 'We thould be ready to shhhart when thish finishhhes. Okay.'

Paul just nodded.

The Buddy Holly track faded away and quite a lot of the dancers suddenly realized that they were not teenagers anymore. Red faced, breathing hard but extremely happy, they flopped down onto their chairs and after a moment grabbed a glass of something cold and downed the lot.

'Wow,' cried Maggie, 'Did I need that. You were fantastic Zoe but my poor feet, they ache like hell.'

'Same here,' said Zoe, 'God, where's Don with my iced lager. I'm gaggin' for another drink. That last one went down without touching me throat.'

20

'Oh, there he is, and he's carrying a tray of drinks, the little darling. Where did you find him?' Maggie grinned, knowing full well that Zoe and Don had been an item since the time they had both left school.

Don had doubled the order to save time at the bar but this meant that the Bingo cards had to be clear of any spilt drinks. Wet cards and marker pens spelt disaster.

Anyway, he had thought of that and produced a handful of drip mats, which he passed around the table.

'What did I tell you Zoe,' winked Maggie. 'A little treasure.'

'Isssh everyone ready.' Wilf tapped his mic a few times. The thump,thump told him that it was working loud and clear.

Paul sat next to him ready to put the ball onto its place on the number check-tray.

"Don't forget to sssshout out as loud asshh you can if you get a line and for a full housshhh we have a ssspeccchhial prize of an organic chicken.'

'Does it play rock and roll,' a wit in the room called out to hoots of laughter and jeers.

'Right, are you ready,' said Wilf grinning, his voice booming around the concert room.

'Here we go then, eyesssh down.'

Holding the mic in one hand, he turned the Bingo cage several times over with the other one and the balls rattled and jumped about inside it. He let go of the cage handle and one fell into a shute and then rolled into a cup.

Wilf picked up the ball, and called out.

'On it's own - Number four' – and then he passed the ball to Paul who placed it in the Ball check-tray as everyone in the room shouted.

'Knock at the door.'

Wilf turned the cage again and then picked up the next ball, calling out –

'All the twossh, twenty-two,' before passing the ball to Paul and the check-tray as the players cried out -

'Two little ducks, Quack, Quack.' ....

4

At the committee table, now set to one side of the hall the Chairman took a sip from his pewter mug, as he looked at the fairly crowded room and said to the club treasurer Fred Notte.

'Pity it took a special meeting to get this lot out. Just think if we had this many three or four times a week.'

'Typical isn't it,' replied Fred.

'The club could go under in a few days and we get this. They're like ghouls at a death, coming out of the woodwork to feast their eyes on the death-throes of it.'

'Oh, come on Fred, it's not that bad, is it?'

'Well, I suppose not. It's just like, you know, I feel that something will go out of the village if we close.'

'I know.' I feel the same too. I've been coming here for over thirty years, nigh on eighteen on the committee would you believe.'

'Aye, time flies and before you know it, you're shaking hands with St Peter at the Pearly Gates.'

'Well, in that case I'm going for another, same again Fred.'

'May as well. At least we're saving fifty pence a pint for the time being aren't we?'

'For God's sake Fred. Cheer-up. You haven't lost your money yet. The witching hour is miles away. I'm sure Chaz Bolton will get in touch soon. I mean Walt has sent a text to him hasn't he?'

'Oh yeah, I saw him do it.'

'So what's the long face for. Hang on while I get these drinks. Okay.'

'LINE.'

The call echoed in the concert room. Steve Woolfe was waving his card in the air. A loud groan went round the room.

'Not him again,' shouted Budd laughing. 'It's a fix I tell you. A fix.'

Paul was already on his way to check the numbers and had the prize ready, a miniature bottle of red wine.

Hoots and catcalls were made as Steve waved the bottle in the air.

'Lucky bastard,' someone yelled. 'Don't drink it all at once.'

Eyesssh down pleashe, eyesssh down,' called Wilf. 'It washh a correct call.' So everyone quietened down as the Bingo cage began to revolve.

The Chairman leaned on the bar, as Barney pulled his order. He was the only one there as the Bingo resumed.

'You know what Barney I shall miss the old place if we do go under. When you think of all that has gone on in the village over the years and the characters that were members. You don't see as many these days you know.'

Barney nodded. He could remember a few characters all right. As he passed over the pewter mug to the Chairman froth foaming over the lip and starting to pull the next pint, he said, 'Talking of characters. Do you remember that silly pillock Owen, the lad that worked on Hill Farm? It was some time back, mind you.'

'I'm not sure,' answered the Chairman taking a drink and wiping some froth from his lips. 'How long ago are you talking about?'

'Oh, it must some ten, fifteen years at least. Don't you remember the hay barn fire at the farm?'

'Ah yes. Our Owen. Quite a lad wasn't he.'

'Aye, he certainly got around with the yobos of the time. Trouble was he was easily led. Some said he wanted to be known as one of the hard cases but everyone knew he was as soft as shit. He did odd jobs at Hill Farm, though how he kept his job is nobody's business. He never did anything right first time round.

Remember when he got a moped and went around dressed in leathers. Everyone took the piss behind his back but he was too thick to notice.'

'Oh, give me a couple of packets of crisps as well, Barney. Cheers pal. You were saying about the Hill Farm fire.'

Barney put the other pint of beer on the bar top and bent down for the crisps.

'Yeah, as I remember, it was late August and most of the hay had been cut and baled and put in the barn. It had been a good warm spell and this night the club was packed out. They were even sitting on the bloody kerb by the bus stop. Chuffin' wonder no one was run over.

Anyway, just after eleven, Owen came dashing into the club shouting his head off, call the police, call the police, the barns on fire, right next to the stables.

Well you could imagine the scene. All hell broke loose.

I phoned the Fire Brigade and then the Police.

Owen said that the farmer had gone over to Lancashire to look at some cattle. He had taken his wife with him and wouldn't be back until late.

Well, half the club ran up to the farm. By the time they got there the Fire Brigade was already at it. But they were too late to save the hay barn though. Some of the lads managed to get the horses out of the stables. Fortunately they were okay. Skittish mind you.

When things quietened down and most people had gone, the club actually stayed open to two or three in the morning. Nobody wanted to go home, not wanting to miss anything; we gave Owen some food and stuff, he was in a bit of a state, dirty face, hair full of straw and mucky clothes. He said he was all right. He had tried to put the fire out on his own, then realized that he needed help.

Everyone said he was a hero and deserved a medal, me included.'

'Hey, where the hell is my pint?' Fred had just come to the bar and sounded a bit put out.

'Oh hell, sorry cock,' said the Chairman, passing it over. 'And have a packet of crisps. I won't be a minute Fred. Barney is just telling me something.'

'Well, next time, let me know you don't want to be a waiter. Okay,' chuntered Fred, as he went back to the table.

'You were saying about Owen, Barney.'

'Oh aye. Would you believe it, the little bastard was arrested for arson two days later. The Fire inspectors looking for the source of the fire had found his wallet in the pigsty, next to two empty petrol cans.'

'Bloody hell, I had forgotten all about that. It was in the local rag for weeks wasn't it.'

'Yeah,' Barney said. 'You remember what the police said about Owen.'

The Chairman shook his head.

Barney held up his hands, 'Owen, they said, wanted to be somebody. Somebody that people would look up to. So he set fire to the barn and ran to the club to give the alarm. The little runt got what he wanted for two days before they copped him. Of course the bugger never came back to Harlston when he got out of clink. Good job too, he probably would have been lynched.'

'Ooops, is that the time. Fred'll kill me. Fill me mug Barney and make it quick please'.

5

'HOUSE'

A big groan came from the rest of the Bingo players.

'I don't believe it,' Budd's voice boomed all round the concert room.

'It's not fixer Steve is it?' he said as friendly catcalls and whistles were made.

Sure enough, Steve Woolfe, face flushed, was on his feet waving a fully marked card. He hadn't won a full house for ages. Well at least for two weeks.

What with his 'Line,' a crappy miniature of red wine but better than nothing, the thirty-five quid on the Bandit and now the organic reared chicken, he felt good.

He thought about the chicken. Hell, he couldn't just leave it lying on his chair could he. What if he went to the bar for a refill. He looked around the room. My God, there are some rum ones in tonight. Must have come from to'ther side of the village. There were always some light-fingered buggers from down there who'd think of nothing of walking off with their 'find'.

He would have to guard the frigging thing all night. God, it was only eight thirty and he needed a few more pints at least to celebrate his wins, didn't he.

Paul came over and called out the marked numbers to Wilf, who agreed that the full card was correct and he went back for the prize.

More catcalls and whistles echoed round the room and then the noises of: 'If only... I only wanted thirty-one... I thought Wilf said... Why the hell doesn't he put his blasted teeth...I couldn't tell what... complain to....'

After handing over the prize, which was in a plastic

Natto carrier bag to Steve, Paul went back to the booth and said to Wilf. 'May as well have the break now, okay.'

Wilf nodded in agreement and made the announcement that there would be a short interval.

Then Paul pushed the button on the CD player.

Anther track from Buddy Holly- *'That'll be the Day'* pulsed out of the speakers.

Many young at heart folk jumped to their feet and filled the gaps between the tables and the small space in front of the stage and began to jive.

Wes Booke took a sip of his compari and spoke to Don Chatts who was watching his wife Zoe gyrating with Maggie to the Buddy Holly music.

'Pardon, what did you say, Wes.'

'I said that this music is appropriate to tonight's meeting isn't it.'

'How do you mean.'

'Well, it's all about saying good-bye isn't it and tonight we're saying it to the club we love.'

Don looked at him and said, 'It's not definite yet, Wes. Wait until the 'Fat Lady' sings. Have you no faith in fate. What is ordained to happen will happen, see. So we wait a bit longer. Then so be it. What's the point of worrying Wes, it's all in the stars. It has already been decided, old cock. Have another drink of your donkey's piss. It might cheer you up,' and he turned and waved to Zoe.

Eric's head was splitting. The blasted drum beat of the Buddy Holly music was like a hammer in his skull. Bang-Bang-Bang, it never seemed to stop.

God, he thought, *I need something to cool it with.*

Idly he look around and at the next table saw Steve Woolfe put his Bingo prize on the chair next to him. It was the frozen organic chicken in a plastic carrier bag.

Eric eyed the bag eagerly. *He could make use of that,* he thought. *If Steve moves away for a drink or maybe a call of nature, he wouldn't miss it for a few minutes would he?*

The thought of an ice-cold chicken pressed to his forehead nearly made Eric faint.

He leaned forward on the table and put his hands on his face, making sure that he could still see the chicken.

Go on Steve, go and have a chuffin' piss. I only want it for a few minutes.

Bang-Bang the sodding drum wouldn't stop. Eric prayed for a miracle to take Steve away.

Maggie Stepp was hot from jiving with Zoe and she waved to her to hang on for a sec.

Standing next to Steve's table, whom she hadn't noticed, she pulled up her T-shirt and wiped her sweaty face. A pair of bra-less well-developed breasts popped into view, just as Steve glanced her way.

He had actually been thinking about having a dance but hadn't made up his mind. He looked again at Maggie in a new light. In her normal Co-op shop tunic she was just another shop assistant. *Hells bells,* he thought *He'd put her in a wet T-shirt any day. Man, who'd have thought it!*

Steve pushed back his chair as another track from Buddy Holly began – 'Oh, Boy!' and limped over to where Zoe and Maggie were dancing.

He had learnt long ago how to adapt his injured gait to rock and roll music. In fact it gave him a certain individual style that impressed the girls. Once he had started to dance it began to work it's magic.

Maggie edged over closer to him.

'Hi, Steve,' she shouted above the music, 'I didn't know you could dance like that.'

'Well,' he laughed, 'It did take me a while to perfect it.' And he did a jump and twirl that made her gasp.

'Wow, that's great Steve. 'Do it again.'

Eric couldn't believe his luck, when he saw Steve get up to dance. A quick look at his mates told him he wouldn't be missed. They were arguing the toss about the merits of rugby league and football.

He managed to stand by holding the back of his chair. Then taking a deep breath, he lurched across to Steve's table and grabbed the plastic Natto bag containing the frozen chicken.

6

Holding the Natto bag close to his chest, *my God how cold it felt,* Eric nearly dropped it; He looked over towards the opposite corner of the stage where a door led to the toilets, a stage dressing-room and a utility room which was where he wanted to go.

Considering how he felt after a few, *that's a laugh,* he thought, drinks, he managed to weave his way past the cavorting jivers quite easily.

Once inside the utility room, (fortunately no one had seen him in the corridor), he switched the light on and closed the door behind him,

In the dingy room packed with odds and sods, he saw an old wooden folding chair with a plastic bowl on the seat full of old cleaning cloths.

Eric kicked the bowl onto the floor and sat down on the wooden chair. Then he lifted the frozen chicken, still inside the plastic shopping bag to his forehead.

Bliss

The shock of the frozen chicken when it touched him cleared his head like magic. The thud, thud of the drum, which was nearly as loud in here as the concert room, was now a pleasant rhythmic beat, he actually began to tap his feet - then he was violently sick – mostly into the shopping bag over the chicken.

Eric dropped the bag to the floor with a loud cry.

'Agh. Oh bloody hell. Steve'll be right pissed off when he sees this lot.'

He wiped his mouth with the back of his hand and picked up an old cloth from the bowl on the floor and cleaned the outside of the Natto bag as best he could.

Shit, he thought, *I'd better get back.* In his hurry to leave he stuffed the cloth on top of the chicken.

Eric pulled the door to the concert room open, and a blast of Oh, Boy! Nearly made Eric drop the Natto bag with its extra 'prize' inside it.

He jigged past the hopping, swaying couples in front of the stage and made his way to Steve's table. His wobbly, jerky walk fitted in quite well with the dancers.

Thank God, the table was still empty. He left the Natto bag on the right chair, he hoped. At that moment the music stopped and a rush of sweaty, thirsty people rushed back for a drink and to flop down on their seats, gasping how great it was to dance to some decent music.

Eric just managed to get back to his own chair first and grabbed hold of his glass and was looking wildly around to see where Steve was, when Wilf Caul's voice boomed out of the PA.

7

Oh Boy! had just faded away when Walt Penn's phone pinged. He took it out of his breast pocket of his sports jacket and read the text message.

He nearly dropped the phone as he turned to the club Chairman.

'Dave, Dave,' he called excitedly.

'It's from Chaz Bolton. He's agreed to the proposal. The deals on, the club's saved.'

Fred Notte the Treasurer butted in, 'Well, well. I'll go to our house. I had a feeling that it might actually fall through because of the way he insisted on us meeting the deadline tonight. Anyway, I'm mighty relieved myself, knowing that my money is safe.'

'Never mind all that,' the Chairman said a big grin on his face.

'It's a big weight off mind I can tell you. I'll go and tell Wilf to let everyone know.'

Fred was only half listening. He had spotted Maggie Stepp going over to Steve Woolfe's table when the music had ended. He wanted to know what was going on between them.

He picked up his pint glass and wondered what to do next

'Attenshon, attenshon. Can I have your attenshon pleash.' Wilf Caul's voice spluttered over the PA system.

'The club Chairman hash jush told me that the club has been bought by Mr Bolton and is shafe.'

As a great cheer went up all over the concert room, Budd leapt up from his chair and ran over to the booth by the stage and whispered something to Paul Flite.

Paul looked up to Budd and grinning said, 'Why not?'

He then pulled a draw open and rifled through a stack of CDs before pulling one out and sliding it into the player. He then hit the play button.

A loud drumbeat was followed by a trumpet trill, which echoed the rhythm – The Conga.

Da-Da-Daaa-Da

Da-Da-Daaa-Da

Budd turned round and yelled, 'Come on, Follow me.'

He had put his hands on his hips and did a 1-2-3, kick to the music and then kept repeating the sequence.

'Come on. Enjoy y'selves,' he shouted.

Zoe Chatts squealed, 'Come on Don,' and she ran to put her hands on Budd's waist, with Don joining her seconds later.

In moments a line of dancers had been formed and were moving in unison, 1-2-3, kick in time to the beat, and with glee.

The line went between the tables along the front of the stage then out of the concert room to the taproom, where it went round the snooker table to the bemused looks of the two players then back to the concert room.

8

When Steve saw Maggie run behind Don he jumped to his feet and managed to get behind her and put his hands on her hips.

She turned to see who it was and smiled when she saw Steve and said, 'Careful where you put your hands big boy,' as she gave him a wink.

Steve winked back and gave her a tight squeeze as Budd led the line of dancers towards the stage.

The club Chairman's phone pinged, so he slipped a hand into his blazer side pocket and pulled it out. He saw that the text was from Barney.

Sorry Dave, the message read. *What with the possibility of the club closing and with the loads of extra Bingo players that have turned up we have run out of beer. The last keg has just run dry. My last order wasn't big enough for tonight's extra sales. Sorry but we're a club with no draught beer.*

'Damn,'

Fred and Walt looked over at the Chairman.

'What's up Dave,' asked Walt.

'You wont believe me if I tell you. We've friggin' run out of beer.'

'How the hell can that be,' asked Fred in a tone that said 'I don't believe it.'

'Well, that was Barney and it's not like him to screw up his brewery orders but I suppose we can't blame him. We all thought that the club was about to close soon didn't we. Anyway, what's done is done. I'd better tell Wilf the bad news. He'll be the one who'll get most of the flak when he announces it. Still he should be used to it. What Bingo caller hasn't had to deal with bad calls before now. Okay lads.'

Walt and Fred nodded.

After the club Chairman had explained the position to them, Paul suggested that it might be better to give it a few more minutes before Wilf made the announcement.

The Chairman agreed but reminded Wilf to thank all the members who had attended the earlier meeting and make sure to say that the committee is really sorry that the club had to close early tonight because of unforeseen circumstances.

9

'I'll just slip to the office then and get my briefcase,' Walt said. 'Before the rush, like.'

The office was a small room set to one side of the club's main entrance.

'Okay,' Fred muttered. He was looking at the conga line and saw Steve holding Maggie a bit more tightly than was necessary for the dance.

Fred's eyes squinted with rage and he said to himself, 'You little prick. I'll get you sorted.'

The conga line had moved to the other side of the concert room, so he eased his way through the mostly empty tables towards Steve's place. All eyes were watching the dance, so no one saw Fred grab the Natto bag with the chicken inside it. He noticed that a piece of cloth had been put over the top of it. *Must be to keep it cool,* he thought, as he walked away with it clutched under one arm.

'Jeez,' he flinched, 'it's damn cold,' he muttered to himself, so he hurried a bit faster to the main entrance and out to the car park.

His car was to one side of the club building, pointing to the main door, which was visible from it. Pressing the remote button, Fred opened a rear door and dropped the Natto bag on the back seat and then climbed into the driving seat and waited.

Paul stopped the CD to loud groans from the dancers but for many it hadn't come a moment too soon. They were knackered though they tried to hide it by false laughter and loud voices as they sat down ready to slake their thirst.

Then Wilf began to blather on about the beer running out and that the committee had reluctantly decided to close the club in a few minutes. He was sorry but that was it. It was out of his hands. Oh and the committee wanted to thank all the ones that had attended the meeting earlier.

'What the hell's going on Wilf,' cried Budd and at least twenty others joined in.

'No more beer ......'

'Shorry but thatsh how it ish,' Wilf boomed back through the PA.

'Good night everybody and have a shafe journey home.'

Those that had a drink left on the table tossed them down pronto, the rest were talking ten to the dozen in loud voices.

Eric had rushed to the bar but was ten seconds too late. Barney had just pulled down the bar security shutters.

'Open the damn shutters Barney, I know you're in there, yelled Eric, banging them with his fists.

'A whiskey will do, I'll buy the friggin' bottle. Come on, Barney, be a sport. I didna hear that. What did you say?'

Eric turned and faced the concert room.

'I think they're closed and I .....'

He slumped to the floor, out cold, his wig curled by his face like a little kitten.

By now most had got the message and were putting on coats and grabbing their Bingo markers and any other personal items.

Calls of good night.... I'll see thee then.... Hang on I've got to make a call...., rang round the room.

The club Chairman was apologizing and saying good night to all and sundry. He had already noticed that Fred and Walt had gone and knew that Paul and Wilf would see to it that the concert room would be left tidy. A proper clean up Barney would see to the next morning.

Maggie had just said, see you to Zoe and Don after saying what a pity it was, closing so early when everyone was having a good time, when Steve came up.

He'd been in the gents when Wilf made his announcement but had heard enough to know the score.

Then she dropped her bombshell.

'Hi, Steve that was great while it lasted wasn't it? Sorry but I have to rush. Fred has promised to run me home. See you around sometime. Okay.'

Steve's smile vanished, 'But, but I.....'

'Have to go, love, see you, bye.'

'Of all the chuffin..... Women,' he cursed angrily as he went back to his table.

'Hey, where's my friggin' chicken?'

Steve looked under the table and the one next to it and then called even louder.

'Anyone seen a Natto bag with a frozen chicken in it?'

Plenty of shaking heads as people walked out of the room

Eric's four mates were just about to pick him up from in front of the bar, where he had collapsed a few minutes before and one looked over to Steve and shouted.

'Maybe it got cold feet and decided to go for a run to warm itself up.'

'Funny guy are you,' and Steve gave him the finger.

'Sod it. I'll never get the bloody thing back. I bet it was one of those yobs from to'ther side of the village,' he chuntered, as he picked up his miniature wine bottle and stuffed it inside his jacket and went to get his car.

Fred couldn't believe his luck when Maggie appeared by herself at the main entrance of the club amongst a gaggle of other people.

He tooted his horn and she turned and waved before coming over.

Fred leaned over to open the far passenger door and Maggie got, in smiling.

'Wow, what a night it's been,' she said breathlessly. 'The club saved; well at least for a fair bit and that dance - the conga, it was great. Did you organize it Fred?'

'Well,' Fred eased over towards her and put one arm round her shoulder.

Maggie lifted up her face and sniffed.

'What the hell is that smell Fred, it's horrible.

Fred took his hand off her shoulder and looked at the bag on the back seat.

Yes there definitely was a funny smell coming from it, though it was only a frozen chicken wasn't it.

He reached over and lifted it over the front seats. The Natto plastic bag split and the frozen chicken covered with Eric's vomit dropped onto Maggie's lap.

'What the hell!'

Then she screamed.

'Fred you bastard. How could you?'

'Maggie, Maggie. I know nothing about it. Honest.'

'I don't chuffin' believe you. You've been looking funny at me all night. Don't think I hadn't noticed.'

'I wasn't, I was looking at....'

'Don't give me excuses. Let me out. I don't want to speak to you again, ever. Do you hear? And get this damn chicken off my legs.'

As soon as Fred had removed it, Maggie jumped out of his car, cursing him to the high heavens.

Then Steve just passing, stopped his car, lowered his window and said.

'Do you want any help Maggie?'

The Author

Watercolour painting

Rita Clements Lee
Also
Lost in France
(A Memoir)

Printed in Great Britain
by Amazon